THE CHICKEN COOP KID

-A SILK FAMILY STORY-

ADAPTED BY KAREN RENEE JOHNSON

ILLUSTRATED BY MATTHEW THAYER

Other Books Available from Loving On Purpose:

❧ for children

Shorts In The Snow by The Silk Family

❧ for parents

Loving Our Kids On Purpose by Danny Silk

Culture Of Honor by Danny Silk

Look for these at
lovingonpurpose.com

This adaptation of
a Silk Family Story
was written by:
Karen Renee Johnson
Illustrations by:
Matt Thayer
Produced by:
Sheri Silk

This book is dedicated to all three of the Silk children.

For many years, they have courageously shared their

lives and stories for the benefit of others. We want to

especially thank Brittney, the "chicken coop kid", for

this very popular story. We love you all beyond words!!

Mom & Dad

One Saturday morning...

Mom shouted to Britt,

"Did you do the dishes?"
nearly having a fit.

"I *will!* I'm going to!"
Brittney replied.

For the past couple days and a five minute chore,
these dishes became an ear *AND* eyesore.

Too busy with homework
and doing her hair,
"I ran out of time,"
Britt said without care.

That's all that mom heard,
but it was enough
to send her to dad
in a huff and a puff.

By this time FLAMES
burst out of Mom's head.
"You look upset,"
Dad wisely said.

"DO SOMETHING!"
Mom said,
her patience
now blown.

So, Dad
went to the sink...

...And washed them up on his own.

Then Brittney bounced in,
all giggly and boppin'
ponytails bouncin',
dolled up to go shoppin'!

"Can I go? Can I go?" was all Britt could say.
"Can I go out shopping with Becca today?"

Dad listened intently,
his hand on his chin.
"Did the dishes for you,"
he said with a grin.

She stopped, jaw dropped, eyes wide to the brim,
"I *was* gonna do 'em!" she said back to him.

"I know," Dad smiled
and gently replied.
"But Dad, that's not fair!"
"Probably so," he sighed.

Britt hemmed
and Britt hawed
as her brain recollected
the last time chores traded...
...and then it connected!

Britt wanted to scream and then run away,
but she knew in her heart she needed to stay.

For a heart connection
was certainly there,
and chores never ruined
the love that they shared.

"Chicken Coop
or trash shed?"
was all that Dad said...

...no screaming
or yelling
or sending to bed.

Becca stood by amazed and in awe
of what she just heard and what she just saw.

So matter-of-factly,
with love in his voice,
Dad spoke and Britt listened...

...completely by
choice!

Britt headed out back to pick out her chore.
She knew what to do since she'd traded before.

The trash shed was buzzin'
with dozens of flies
who flew in her face
when she peeked inside.

"Oh, GROSS!" Britt yelled, breathing into her
sleeve.
The smell of the trash made her just want to
heave!

In utter disgust,
towards the chickens Britt headed,
Wishing they all were
fried, baked or breaded.

"OOOH *GROSS!* SILLY CHICKENS!
Get out of the way!"

"What are you *DOING?*"
was all Becca could say.

Britt came back to the house
and chose: "chicken pen."
"Thank you," Dad said,
"Now let's talk about when."

Dad gave her a choice
- do it now or tomorrow -
and her countenance changed
from one of great sorrow...

"Can I still go out shopping
with Becca today?"
With a nod and a hug,
Dad gave his okay!

The next day was rainy
and Dad was sure stoked
Britt chose to trade chores
and *HE* wouldn't get soaked!

Britt walked on by trying
not to be seen,
hoping Dad would forget
what had to be cleaned.

"Hey Britt,
want my raincoat?"
Dad asked with a grin.
"Go ahead and use it
since I'm staying in."

Britt headed outside
to the damp chicken coop
to shovel the stinky and wet
chicken poop.

It was *SMELLY* and AWFUL!
Chickens got in her way,

and feathers were **FLYING** as she shoveled the hay.

By the time she was done
three hours had passed
when Brittney showed
up at the slider at last.

Pitchfork in her hand
and straw in her hair,
a dripping, exhausted
Brittney stood there!

Britt headed off for a much needed shower
frustrated this chore had taken

THREE HOURS!!

A couple days later, words echoed the hall,...

...the very same words that had started it all.

"**B**ritt, do the dishes,"
Mom gracefully asked.

Brittney's response was,
"I *WILL!*" to this task.

Dad stood right up
and cheerfully announced,
"I'll get 'em Britt,"
but she rose with a bounce.

Britt flew through the room
declaring her wishes,
jumping the sofa,
"Get away from *MY* dishes!"

The End

The Silk Family

This true story is adapted from a teaching series by Danny Silk called
Loving Our Kids On Purpose.

For more information about Danny and Sheri Silk
or any other products by Loving on Purpose please visit:

lovingonpurpose.com

Story adapted by: Karen Renee Johnson

Karen Renee Johnson is a freelance writer and poet who has been writing rhymes and stories since she was ten years old. Her passion for parenting with Freedom and Joy inspired her to begin a series of children's books based on Danny's humorous stories from *Loving Our Kids On Purpose*. Karen lives in Redding, California, with her husband and their two little geniuses.

karenreneejohnson.com

Illustrations by: Matthew Thayer

Matthew Thayer and his wife, Joy, live in Redding, CA with their children. He has been drawing cartoons since he was two years old and has a profound love for creativity and the arts. In addition to illustrating, Matthew is a writer who is working on several screenplays as well as co-authoring a series of children's novels with Joy. He also draws and co-writes *The LOP-Side*, a comic strip for lovingonpurpose.com.

Other Books Available from Loving On Purpose:

❧ <u>for children</u>

Shorts in the Snow by The Silk Family

❧ <u>for parents</u>

Loving Our Kids On Purpose by Danny Silk

Culture Of Honor by Danny Silk

Look for these at
lovingonpurpose.com

Made in the USA
Lexington, KY
08 January 2016